# A Pig Tale

# A Pig Tale

By Olivia Newton-John
and Brian Seth Hurst
Illustrated by Sal Murdocca

SIMON & SCHUSTER BOOKS FOR YOUNG READERS
Published by Simon & Schuster
New York • London • Toronto • Sydney • Tokyo • Singapore

SIMON & SCHUSTER BOOKS FOR YOUNG READERS
Simon & Schuster Building, Rockefeller Center
1230 Avenue of the Americas, New York, New York 10020

Designed by David Neuhaus.
The text of this book is set in 15 pt. Goudy Old Style.
The illustrations were done in watercolor.
Manufactured in the United States of America

10  9  8  7  6  5  4  3  2  1

Library of Congress Cataloging-in-Publication Data
Newton-John, Olivia. A pig tale / by Olivia Newton-John and Brian Seth Hurst ;
illustrated by Sal Murdocca.   p.   cm.
Summary: Ziggy proudly invites other piglets and their parents to
see what his father has made from all the things he has been saving.
[1. Recycling (Waste)—Fiction.   2. Pigs—Fiction.   3. Fathers and sons—Fiction.
4. Stories in rhyme.]   I. Hurst, Brian Seth.
II. Murdocca, Sal, ill.   III. Title.
PZ8.3.N523Pi  1993  [E]—dc20  92-44116  CIP
ISBN: 0-671-78778-0

This book is printed on recycled paper.

For my darling Chloe and her friend Colette
who loved animals so much
O. N-J.

For Katie and Kenny
B. H.

For Alan Benjamin
S. M.

Now here's a strange pig tale
that's written in rhyme
of Ziggy, Pop Iggy, and
*Once upon a time.*

Now some pigs like garbage,
and most pigs love slop;
but no other pig was like
Ziggy's old pop.

He saved and collected
'most any old thing,
from biscuits to baskets
to miles of old string.

From cans to flat tires
to old paper bags,
to sofas and soupspoons,
to old clothes and rags.

From rubber bands, golf balls,
and horns from old Jeeps
to whatchamacallits
and bleepity-bleeps.

The house was a mess.
It was filled to the top,
but Iggy kept saving.
He just couldn't stop.

The piglets at school
would all giggle and grump,

and tell little Ziggy
he lived in a dump.

One day from the barn
Ziggy heard such a clatter,
he banged on the door, shouting,
"Pop, what's the matter?"

But Iggy told Ziggy,
"Go play and have fun.
Don't worry, I'll call you
when my work is done."

His daddy kept hammering:
*Bang, Batter, Zip, Zing.*
He was working so hard
on a most special thing.

Ziggy told all his friends
of his father's surprise,
and to come with their parents
to await the sunrise.

As night turned to dawn,
the noises just stopped,
and Ziggy stepped forward
to welcome his pop.

The door opened wide
and everyone stared,
but no one could speak—
not a single pig dared.

Then what they all saw
made them cheer,
dance, and sing:
"An amazing invention!"
"A most beautiful thing!"

A big ball of color,
of canvas and string,
of tires and tubas,
of every old thing.

It gleamed and it glittered,
as round as the moon;

Iggy's brilliant creation:
a wondrous balloon!

Then Iggy took Ziggy
up high for a ride,
and Ziggy was proud
to be by his side.

They circled the globe
in their beautiful ball,
and his pop was a hero
to Ziggy and all.

Now here is the reason
for telling this tale:
Let's save the world's treasures,
from tin can to whale.

Protect our dear earth.
Don't throw it away.
You, too, could make magic
from garbage someday.